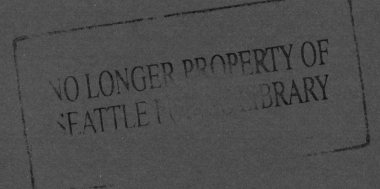

For Kendall and Archie:
beasts big and small

Little Doctor
and the
Fearless Beast

by
Sophie Gilmore

Owlkids Books

There once lived a child the crocodiles called Little Doctor.

The creatures came from
all around to see her.

And Little Doctor treated
each one with care.

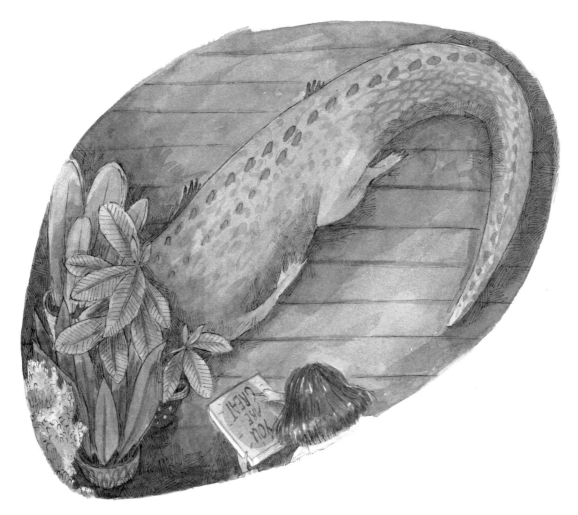

As she worked, she
admired their tough armor
and large, powerful jaws.

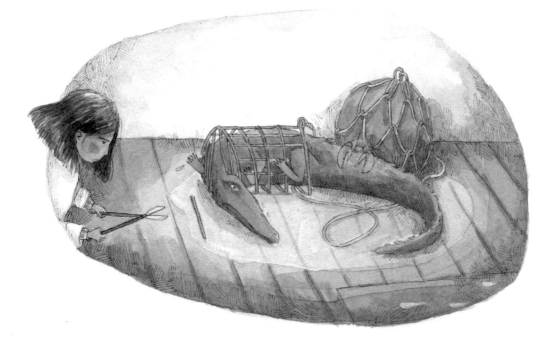

In exchange for her kindness, the crocodiles told Little Doctor tales. Each legend teemed with terrible danger, dizzying escapes, and acts of great mischief.

Little Doctor marveled at the fearless beasts they described.

One day, such a legendary beast arrived.
Little Doctor had heard whispers of her.

Big Mean was the biggest in the land, with stony eyes and jaws large enough to devour Little Doctor in one fell swoop. But today, her mouth was clamped shut.

Little Doctor examined Big Mean for bruises, scrapes, or broken bones, keeping a wary eye on those jaws. The crocodile's eyes followed her every move, making Little Doctor feel as though she were the one being examined.

Big Mean *seemed* fine. Perhaps it was a fever? Little Doctor approached the beast with a thermometer to pop under her tongue.

But Big Mean
did not like that.
Not one bit.

Little Doctor
tried again.

And again.

As Little Doctor grew
more determined to help,

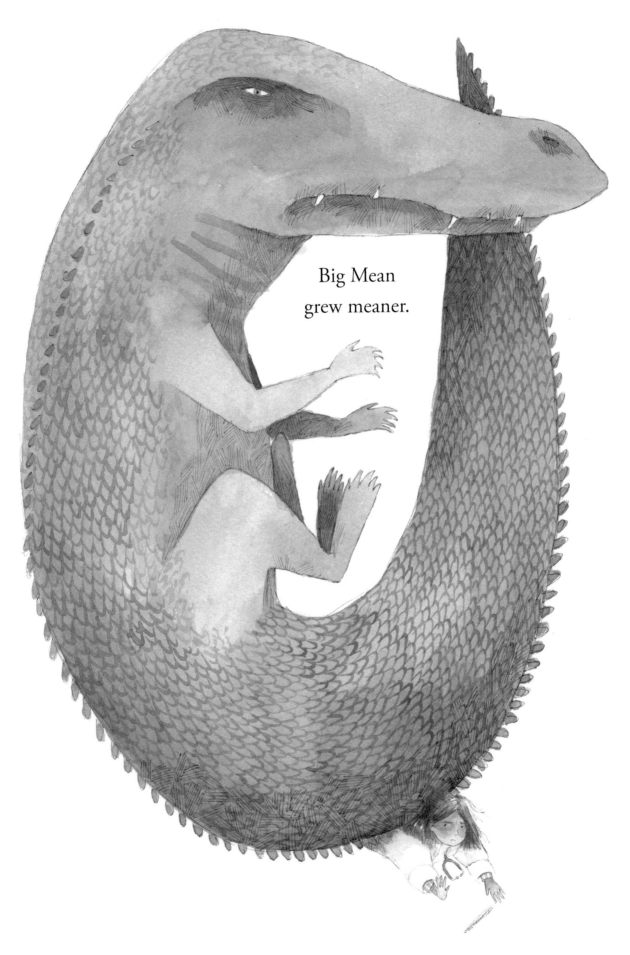

Big Mean
grew meaner.

Little Doctor retreated, feeling tired and cross. "Why are you here?" she muttered rather loudly. She returned to her other patients, her temper soothed by her work.

As Big Mean watched Little Doctor's tenderness toward her fellow crocodiles, something inside her softened. She closed her eyes and drifted off into a doze.

Little Doctor noticed the great beast resting and
an idea took hold. She found a volunteer, and they
sprang into action.

The plan was going well until—

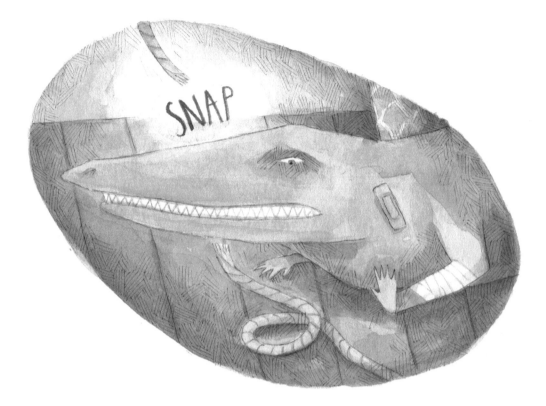

Little Doctor tumbled through the air.

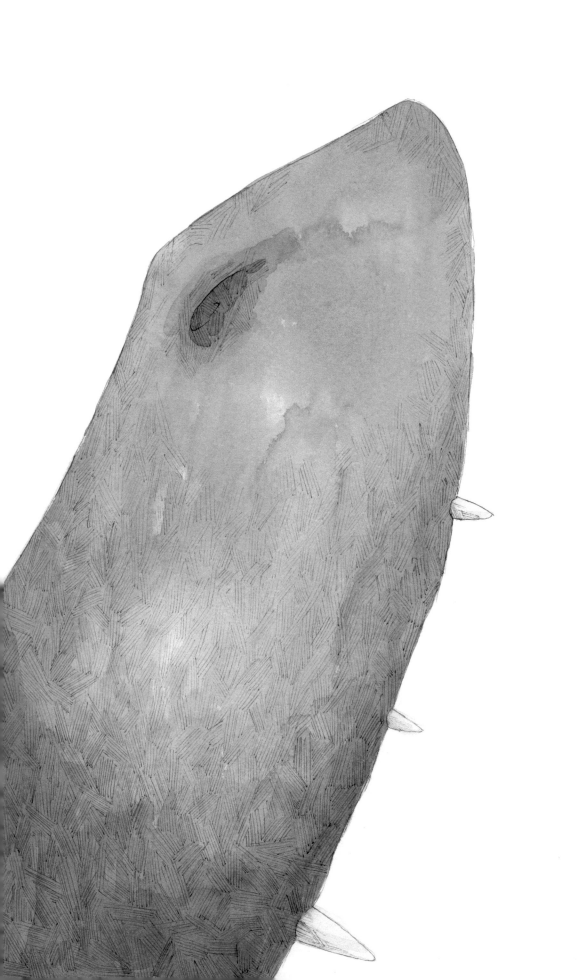

In that instant, Big Mean's eyes flashed.
She finally opened her tremendous jaws
wide, wide as a river…

and Little Doctor

       fell

        right

      in.

Little Doctor shut her eyes tight,
expecting to be munched
or crunched.

But moments passed,
and she was not munched
nor crunched.

Instead she heard a small

CHIRP.

She opened her eyes.

And she
understood.

Little Doctor worked quickly to untangle the
hatchlings. Her small hands were nimble where
Big Mean's large claws must have fumbled.

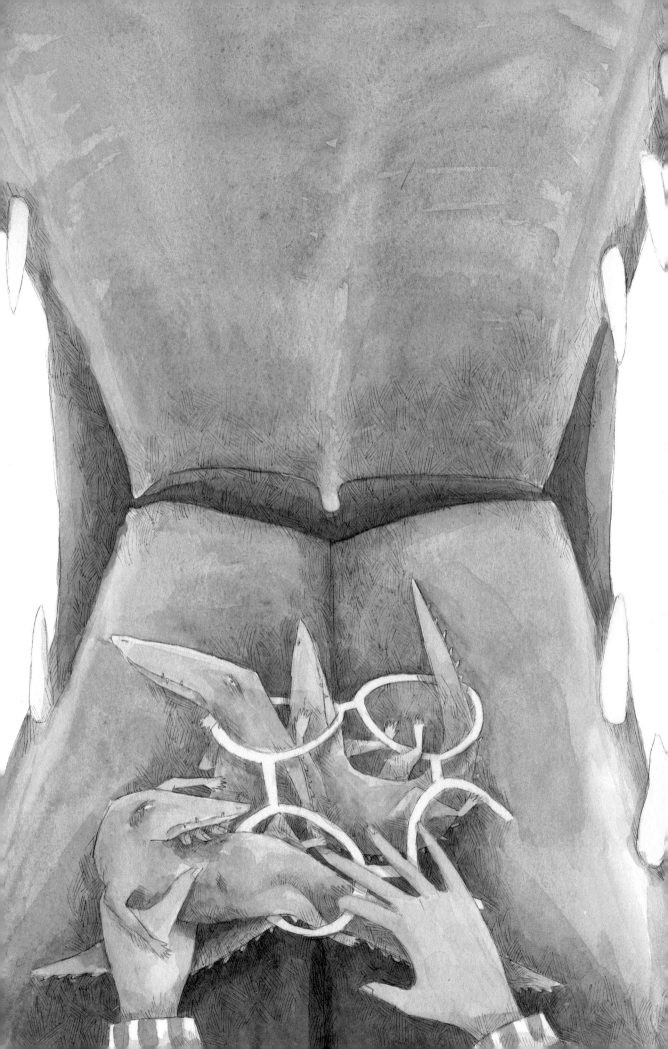

Little Doctor and the others gathered around Big Mean. What tale would she share? Big Mean spoke, and her voice was strong and loud. "This is an important story, a story of great daring and determination."

Big Mean's eyes twinkled. "It is the tale of the fearless beast, Little Doctor, who could not rest until she had helped her fellow creature. Even a big mean one."

The crocodiles whooped, and Little Doctor glowed.
I am a fearless beast, she whispered to herself.

And together they danced until it was a new day.

Owlkids Books acknowledges the financial support of the Canada Council for the Arts,
the Ontario Arts Council, the Government of Canada through the Canada Book Fund (CBF)
and the Government of Ontario through the Ontario Creates Book Initiative
for our publishing activities.

Published in Canada by
Owlkids Books Inc.
1 Eglinton Avenue East
Toronto, ON M4P 3A1

Published in the US by
Owlkids Books Inc.
1700 Fourth Street
Berkeley, CA 94710

Library of Congress Control Number: 2018946404

Library and Archives Canada Cataloguing in Publication

Gilmore, Sophie (Sophie Lorna Jamieson), author, illustrator
Little Doctor and the fearless beast / by Sophie Gilmore.

ISBN 978-1-77147-344-6 (hardcover)
I. Title.

PZ7.1.G55Lit 2019   j823'.92   C2018-903433-5

Edited by: Karen Li
Designed by: Alisa Baldwin

Manufactured in Shenzhen, Guangdong, China, in May 2019, by WKT Co. Ltd.
Job #19CB0454

B   C   D   E   F   G

ONTARIO ARTS COUNCIL
CONSEIL DES ARTS DE L'ONTARIO
an Ontario government agency
un organisme du gouvernement de l'Ontario

Canada Council   Conseil des Arts
for the Arts   du Canada

Canada

Publisher of Chirp, Chickadee and OWL
www.owlkidsbooks.com

Owlkids Books is a division of 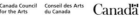 bayard canada